IN A DARK WOOD

Blerime Topalli &
Peter Stass

13HORROR.COM BOOKS
An imprint of
DIZZY EMU PUBLISHING
1714 N McCadden Place, Hollywood, Los Angeles 90028
dizzyemupublishing.com

In A Dark Wood
Blerime Topalli and Peter Stass

ISBN: 9798786859172

First published in the United States
in 2021 by 13Horror.com Books/Dizzy Emu Publishing

1 3 5 7 9 10 8 6 4 2

IN A DARK WOOD

Blerime Topalli &
Peter Stass

EXT. FOREST - DAWN

EASTERN EUROPE - 1945

A winter chilled forest. German army boots CRUNCH through
the snow. Two vicious GERMAN SHEPHERDS pull at their
leads as six rag-tag SOLDIERS give chase.

A GIRL (12) runs frantically through the thicket in a
white nightgown. JUERGEN and DIETRICH (early 20s), a
brutal pair, release their dogs on her.

CAPTAIN BROCHAUER (45), sensible, iron-jawed leader,
reaches them too late to stop them. Frustrated, he
heightens the pace as the two men CACKLE FIENDISHLY.

EXT. VILLAGE WALLS - DAWN

The Girl barely reaches the walls, climbing desperately,
but is taken down by both dogs as she CRIES OUT in vain.

Brochauer reaches the Girl, flinging the dogs off of her.
Juergen and Dietrich STOP LAUGHING, angered as the dogs
YELP in pain. The Girl lays blood-spattered and
unconscious.

GOTTESMAN, 18, with a stereotypical Aryan and angelic
visage, watches the snow fall. A perfect flake lands on
his cheek and melts like a tear. He smiles.

                    BROCHAUER
          Ludwig! The girl's badly hurt. Carry her
          inside.

LUDWIG (30), the medic, is incredulous.

                    LUDWIG
          She's a dirty gypsy. What makes you think
          I'd waste good medical supplies on her--

                    BROCHAUER
          I am your Captain and it's an order -
          that's why.

                    JUERGEN
          Forgive me, *Captain*, but we're in the
          middle of a war--

                    BROCHAUER
          This war is nearly over Juergen, don't
          worry. As for this predicament, we
          wouldn't be here if you had any self-
          control.
                    (MORE)

                    BROCHAUER (CONT'D)
          She is a little girl for godssakes. Now
          which one of you will carry her in?

He looks around at the men:

MOUSE (23), shrugs helplessly; he can barely hold up his
own gun, much less a girl.

Juergen and Dietrich are defiant.

Brochauer turns to Gottesman, still watching the snow
like a child, and SIGHS.

Brochauer picks up the Girl and sets off for the entrance
to the village. His men follow.

EXT. VILLAGE ENTRANCE - CONTINUOUS

Once inside, they notice cottages and thatch roofed huts
dotting a small town square against a backdrop of stark,
sheer mountains.

Shutter doors SLAM shut.

                    BROCHAUER
                 (calling out)
          My name is Captain Brochauer! We are
          members of the 100th Jäger Division of
          his Furor's Wehrmacht Heer!
                 (beat)
          We have a girl, one of your own. She's
          injured.

Another shutter CLAPS shut.

                    BROCHAUER (CONT'D)
          We mean you no harm, but this girl must
          have medical attention immediately! Her
          parents--

Just then a door opens, and an OLD MAN (60s) appears in
the doorway.

                    BROCHAUER (CONT'D)
          You! Old Man!
                 (starting towards him)
          Does this child belong to you?

He is silent. Brochauer's men push past him, into the
house.

INT. OLD MAN'S COTTAGE - CONTINUOUS

It is simple. A bedroom and a kitchen. A chair rests
beside a CRACKLING hearth.

The Old Man barely flinches as the men tear through his
home and ransack the kitchen for food.

He takes the Girl from Brochauer and sets her down in the
chair.

                    BROCHAUER
          Ludwig!

Ludwig stops rummaging through a cabinet.

                    BROCHAUER (CONT'D)
          You will dress her wounds now.

                    LUDWIG
          But Captain, we're starving!

                    BROCHAUER
          NOW!

Ludwig peevishly takes out some supplies and goes over to
dress the girl's wounds.

He stops suddenly, staring in shock.

ANGLE ON WOUND HALF HEALED

                    LUDWIG (O.C.)
          Extraordinary... she's already healing.

Brochauer puts his hand to her forehead. Her eyes pop
open and her BREATHING BECOMES ERRATIC.

                    GIRL
          Li'sa'eer! Eshte baxt amaro gav eshte
          corthu!

                    BROCHAUER
          Mouse!

                    MOUSE
             (rushing over)
          Yes, Captain.

                    BROCHAUER
          You studied linguistics at the Seminary,
          didn't you?

                              MOUSE
                Well... I studied Latin, Aramaic--

                              BROCHAUER
                But you learned some of the local
                language on your last tour.

                              MOUSE
                A little... or at least we tried.

                              BROCHAUER
                The snow's getting heavier. We're not
                going anywhere tonight. If we can
                communicate with them, maybe we can find
                out where their food is.

                              THE GIRL
                Kal'enedral shena... ayo eshte ves'tacha!

                              MOUSE
                Well, it seems like some sort of obscure
                local dialect. I'm not sure, though...
                she's mumbling...

Mouse leans in close to listen. Her back arches, eyes
widening, GASPING. Mouse backs away. The Girl returns to
her MUMBLING.

                              MOUSE (CONT'D)
                     (shrugs)
                Perhaps Albanian mixed with Sinti or
                Roma, I'm not sure.

                              LUDWIG
                I don't think she'll make it through the
                night. If the wound didn't kill her, the
                fever surely will.

Brochauer looks at her small, pale face with sympathy.

Mouse kneels beside her to pray.

                              MOUSE
                Almighty, Everlasting God, the eternal
                Salvation of them that believe: Hear our
                prayers on behalf of Thy servants who are
                sick, for whom we implore the aid of Thy
                mercy--

Juergen dumps dish-ware out of a cabinet with a CRASH!

                              JUERGEN
                Sinti? Praying for a bunch of dirty
                Gypsies. Look at him--

Juergen nods towards the Old Man, who calmly puts a cold
rag on the girl's forehead.

                    JUERGEN (CONT'D)
          The heathen doesn't even know you are
          praying for his filthy little brat!

Dietrich walks up to the Old Man and leans in close.

                    DIETRICH
          Or maybe he's a Jew. Only a Jew would be
          too stingy to pray for his own child.

Brochauer pushes Dietrich away from him.

                    BROCHAUER
          Does imagining her to be a Jew, or a
          Gypsy make it easier for you to kill
          children, Dietrich? Or is it something in
          your **own** nature?

Dietrich backs away and stares at Brochauer in contempt.

                    JUERGEN
          With respect, Captain, we are starving
          and yet you defend these animals instead
          of the Reich--

Brochauer gets in his face.

                    BROCHAUER
          I've made and broken hundreds of better
          men than you and led them to their deaths
          in this filthy war! Don't speak to me
          about the Reich. There are no men in the
          Reich.
                    (beat)
          We are all that's left.

Juergen barely contains his hatred as Brochauer steps
past him. Mouse quietly retreats to fiddle with the
broken radio transmitter.

                    BROCHAUER (CONT'D)
          That can wait, Mouse. They must be hiding
          a store of supplies somewhere in the
          village to get them through the winter.
          We'll pair off and go house to house.

Juergen and Dietrich exchange a blood-thirsty look.

                    BROCHAUER (CONT'D)
          Ludwig, you'll stay with the girl.

                    LUDWIG
          With all due respect, sir, we are wasting
          our supplies on a corpse--

Brochauer ignores him as he buttons his coat.

Gottesman stares out the front door, lost in his own
world.

                    BROCHAUER
          It's cold out, Gottesman. Put your gloves
          back on.

EXT. VILLAGE SQUARE - LATER

A large ancient bell lies broken in the center of the
square. Brochauer leans against it as he chews an unlit
cigar, overseeing the search.

The townspeople are gathered behind him, watching
silently as their homes are ransacked, betraying no
emotion.

INT. COTTAGE #2 - CONTINUOUS

Mouse searches behind some bookcases as Gottesman wanders
aimlessly about.

                    GOTTESMAN
          ...the Visigoths first invaded the Balkan
          Peninsula in 268 AD. It was only after
          their defeat in the battle of Naissus
          that they retreated from the region and
          became known as Aryans, a branch of
          Christianity that was in opposition to
          the Catholic Trinity--

                    MOUSE
          Yes, yes, Gottesman. Now please stop
          talking and make yourself useful!

Mouse finds a loose floorboard and pries it out. His eyes
widen as he lifts a strange and elaborate looking TOME
from the shadows and webs.

EXT. VILLAGE SQUARE - CONTINUOUS

The Villagers TURN THEIR FACES IN UNISON toward Cottage
#2. Brochauer sees this.

Juergen and Dietrich exit another dwelling, frustrated.
Dietrich throws a child's doll to the ground and SMASHES
it with his boot.

Brochauer LIGHTS his cigar and turns away in anger.

Mouse hurries from the thatch hut with the tome in hand.
The Villagers follow him with their gaze.

                    MOUSE
          Captain!

Mouse opens the book, revealing illuminated text written
in a strange alphabet, and archaic images.

                    MOUSE (CONT'D)
          It looks like a history of the village,
          perhaps a sacred text, like a Bible. But
          it's not religious as far as I can tell.

Brochauer glances at it with disinterest.

                    BROCHAUER
          And how is this going to help us eat?
          Even if this storm lets up, it may take
          days to navigate out of these mountains
          and rendezvous with our ground troops. We
          need food.

                    MOUSE
          You want to know about their language?
          Communicate with them? Look--

He points to the strange lettering.

                    MOUSE (CONT'D)
          Aramaic lettering. Their language is a
          combination of some Roma, yes, and
          certainly Albanian, the local language.
          But it contains a great deal of Aramaic,
          which is highly unusual.

                    BROCHAUER
          Will you be able to talk to them?

                    MOUSE
          Perhaps... I'll try to speak to the Old
          Man. But it seems they are in worse shape
          than we are as far as food. The tome is
          probably their most valuable item.

Brochauer examines the images more closely, particularly
the SCENE OF A TERRIBLE PLAGUE.

Suddenly, Juergen grabs the tome from Mouse.

                    JUERGEN
          If we can't eat it, I don't care.

He throws it on the ground.

Suddenly a VILLAGE MAN (60's) rushes to retrieve it.

Dietrich crushes his hand beneath his boot, then picks up
the tome and RIPS it in half. He LAUGHS at the Village
Man, who shakes with pain and anger.

Brochauer throws his cigar into the snow.

Juergen picks up a rock and walks over to the rusted
bell. CLANG! CLANG! CLANG!

                    JUERGEN (CONT'D)
          FOOD! Understand, you heathens? Food!

The Villagers react to the sound of the bell with
ANGUISH, covering their ears and turning away.

Dietrich LAUGHS. Brochauer grabs him from behind in a
choke hold.

                    BROCHAUER
          Release him. Now!

Juergen starts for Brochauer, but then remembers his
place. Dietrich relents. The Village Man climbs to his
feet, rubbing his injured hand.

Brochauer lets go of Dietrich and picks up the torn book.

                    BROCHAUER (CONT'D)
          Mouse.

                    MOUSE
          Yes, Captain.

                    BROCHAUER
          Take this to the cottage. Rebind it after
          you finish fixing the radio.

Mouse looks at Brochauer, uneasily. It's a strange
request.

                    MOUSE
          Yes, Captain.

He takes the tome and heads off to the cottage. Brochauer
takes out a fresh cigar and starts to light it.

                    JUERGEN
          The Reich should have retired you.

Brochauer stops.

                    JUERGEN (CONT'D)
          You were once a hero to soldiers like me.
          I watched you receive the iron cross from
          the Fuhrer himself... now you're just an
          old man, gone soft.

Disgusted, Juergen heads toward the Old Man's cottage,
Dietrich following.

Gottesman emerges from the thatch dwelling, BABBLING.

                    GOTTESMAN
          There are no forks, or knives here,
          Captain. You know the fork was only
          introduced to Europe in the 11th century
          as a novelty, and only came in common use
          in the early 1800's...

Brochauer gently leads Gottesman towards the cottage.

EXT. OLD MAN'S COTTAGE - CONTINUOUS

Snow falls softly. Two dog leads are tethered to a post,
but their chain collars lie empty in the snow. The dogs
are gone.

Mouse stares at the post, hugging the tome closely. He
hears someone approach and retreats to the doorway.

Juergen and Dietrich appear, angered at the sight of the
empty collars.

                    JUERGEN
          Where are they?!

                    MOUSE
          I don't know...

They push him aside and thrust the door open.

INT. OLD MAN'S COTTAGE - CONTINUOUS

As Juergen and Dietrich storm in, Ludwig is startled
awake in the chair by the hearth. The Girl remains
fevered and semi-conscious.

Juergen grabs Ludwig by the collar.

                    JUERGEN
          Where are my dogs?!

                    LUDWIG
          Ju-Juergen, I didn't--

Juergen unholsters his pistol and points it at his face.
CLACK! He cocks it.

                    JUERGEN
          You lazy cow, you couldn't keep your eyes
          open for two minutes to stop these rotten
          villagers from letting my dogs loose?!

                    LUDWIG
          Please, Juergen, I had nothing to do with
          it! I was tired, I'm starving--

Juergen SWATS him with the gun, GASHING his cheek with
BLOOD. The Girl writhes, as if reacting to it.

Brochauer and Gottesman arrive at open door.

                    BROCHAUER
          Put down your weapon!

Juergen stubbornly keeps his gun aimed at Ludwig.
Dietrich watches, shifting nervously, unsure what to do.

                    BROCHAUER (CONT'D)
          That's an order!

No response. Brochauer points his gun at Juergen's head.

                    DIETRICH
          Captain! They took our dogs! He was
          sleeping at his post--

                    BROCHAUER
          You are in violation of a direct order
          from a superior officer!
                    (lower, cold)
          If you do not stop this mutiny, I will.

Brochauer COCKS his gun. A tense beat. Juergen relents.

                    JUERGEN
          I don't need to waste the bullet anyway.

Brochauer takes his pistol away from him.

                    BROCHAUER
          Your rifle.

Juergen reluctantly hands it to him.

> BROCHAUER (CONT'D)
> (to Deitrich)
> You as well. Ludwig may be pathetic, but
> he's still worth more than a dog!

Dietrich is appalled, but he does as he's told.

> BROCHAUER (CONT'D)
> I'm sure they simply escaped from their
> leads and will return when they're
> hungry.

> JUERGEN
> They're already hungry. We all are.

> BROCHAUER
> You are of no use with the villagers. You
> will remain here until you can follow
> orders.

Juergen and Dietrich sit down, chastised.

> BROCHAUER (CONT'D)
> Mouse, you will continue with the repair
> of our radio, then the tome. Ludwig, I
> trust you will stay awake.

Ludwig frowns, humiliated, and checks on the Girl.

> BROCHAUER (CONT'D)
> Gottesman and I will conduct a survey of
> the surrounding area. Perhaps we'll
> stumble across some supplies.

Gottesman lingers outside the front door, staring at the
sky as a snowflake falls on his outstretched tongue.

> GOTTESMAN
> Snowflakes are condensed water droplets
> which always form into hexagonal, six-
> armed crystals. Always six. This is due
> to the geometry of water-crystals...

> BROCHAUER
> Yes, Gottesman, let's go take a look at
> those snowflakes. Shall we?

He leaves the men to settle in uneasily with one another.

EXT. FIELD - LATER

Brochauer and Gottesman walk the village fields, the
afternoon light dimmed by heavy clouds.

Brochauer sees a plow, caked with snow. He wipes it off
to examine it.

                    GOTTESMAN
               (mumbling)
          Never used.

                    BROCHAUER
          What's that?

                    GOTTESMAN
          On my family's farm we would have never
          left a plow in the snow.

He kneels, digging through the snow and into the dirt. He
tastes it.

                    GOTTESMAN (CONT'D)
          This field is dead.

                    BROCHAUER
          Dead?

                    GOTTESMAN
          It has not been used in years. The earth
          is... dead.

Brochauer looks across the field and sees the tip of a
spire poking out from behind tall pines. He starts toward
it as Gottesman trails behind.

                    GOTTESMAN (CONT'D)
          In the fall we grew apples, pears,
          grapes, mulberries, lingonberries...

INT. OLD MAN'S COTTAGE - CONTINUOUS

Mouse fiddles with the radio, then puts it down in favor
of the tome. He picks it up and turns the pages, MOUTHING
OUT several of the Aramaic words.

Ludwig watches with disgust as the Old Man gently places
a cold compress to his grand-daughter's cheek. She
writhes in discomfort.

His feet propped on the kitchen table, Dietrich stares at
the Old Man as he deliberately whittles a piece of wood
to a sharp point. Juergen leans sourly against the wall.

                    JUERGEN
          This is ridiculous. We should be looking
          for the dogs instead of sitting here like
          school children.

Dietrich throws the piece of wood down and rises.

                    DIETRICH
          I'm with you.

                    MOUSE
          Captain Brochauer told us...

His VOICE TRAILS OFF as Juergen approaches menacingly,
grabbing the tome before Mouse can protest.

                    JUERGEN
          And **you** should be working on the radio,
          shouldn't you?
                    (leaning in)
          But maybe a 'Mouse' like you would like
          us all to stay here, away from the war,
          all safe and cozy. Maybe that radio isn't
          broken at all.

Juergen raises the book over Mouse's head threateningly.
Mouse cringes as Dietrich SNICKERS.

                    LUDWIG
          Why don't you stop your bullying,
          Juergen? Everyone is tired of watching
          Brochauer put you in your place.

Juergen ignores him, holding the book above the hearth.
The Girl's eyes pop open, and the Old Man turns to gaze
at Juergen chillingly.

Slowly, Juergen brings the book closer to the fire. The
Old Man sneers, but turns his attention back to the Girl.

Juergen SNICKERS and drops the book back in front of
Mouse with a THUMP!

                    JUERGEN
                    (to Ludwig and Mouse)
          You're a waste to the Reich. We'll be
          back with our dogs. Tell that to the
          Captain when he returns.

Dietrich SMIRKS as the two leave the cottage.

EXT. CHURCH GRAVEYARD - CONTINUOUS

Brochauer and Gottesman walk an overgrown cemetery,
tombstones jutting out askew. Forest pines grow tall in
their midst, making the area seem long lost.

Brochauer stops at a gravestone. He removes some dead
leaves to reveal the year of death - 1534. He looks at
several more and sees the same. Again and again, 1534.

                    GOTTESMAN
          Thirteen.

Brochauer is startled.

                    GOTTESMAN (CONT'D)
          One, plus five, plus three, plus four.
          Thirteen.
                    (beat)
          Did you know that the number thirteen is
          considered bad luck in western culture
          due to the slaughter of the Knights
          Templar by Pope Innocent on Friday the
          13th? However, in the Jewish culture,
          it's considered good luck...

Brochauer relaxes a bit at the familiarity of Gottesman's
madness, but lingers on the tombstones for a beat before
heading toward the church. Gottesman follows, MUMBLING.

EXT. VILLAGE WALLS - DUSK

Snow falls much harder now. Juergen and Dietrich trudge
through eerie semi-darkness, WHISTLING for their dogs.

There's a SNAP in the brush a few yards away. Juergen
holds up his hand for silence and GESTURES toward it.

Another CRACK in the opposite direction. The men turn
toward it. Juergen goes for his weapon instinctively, but
grabs his shoulder to find nothing. Dietrich feels his
empty holster. His hands TREMBLE.

The men stand back to back, facing out to the wilderness.
Another NOISE... the WHINING of dogs close-by.

                    JUERGEN
          The dogs!

They turn towards the WHINING, WHISTLING for the animals.

One of the Shepherds, UTA, apears. She looks tired, head sunken low, eyes empty and mouth frothing. She alternates between WHIMPERING and a LOW GROWL.

Dietrich squats down and inches toward her.

                    DIETRICH
          That's a good girl... Come, Uta. Come.

He gets closer as she GROWLS, baring her fangs. Suddenly, she changes her mind and licks his fingers.

Dietrich turns to LAUGH at Juergen, who LAUGHS back.

Suddenly--BRUNO, the other Shepherd, LEAPS on Dietrich, TEARING into his neck. He falls to his knees, blood SPURTING from his jugular.

                    DIETRICH (CONT'D)
          Help!! Juergen, HELP!!!

Juergen is frozen, in shock. Both dogs now turn on Dietrich, mauling him.

Juergen stumbles backward, then runs off in terror.

The dogs give chase, leaving Dietrich to bleed to death.

Juergen's steps are clumsy. PANICKED BREATHING, as the dogs leap expertly through the trees after him.

EXT. VILLAGE WALLS - CONTINUOUS

Juergen almost makes it to the village wall, but slips and looks back to see the hounds closing in. He scrambles up and almost gains the wall, but it's too late. Uta sinks her teeth into his leg and takes him down. Both dogs tear into Juergen as he SCREAMS.

INT. OLD MAN'S COTTAGE - SAME TIME

Mouse holds the tome, chewing on a pencil as he tries to decipher the text. He HEARS Juergen's SCREAM and jumps, dropping the tome on the floor.

Ludwig awakens, sitting up in his chair. The Old Man stops stoking the fire to listen, then returns to it as the SCREAM TRAILS OFF.

                    LUDWIG
          What was that?!

                    MOUSE
          We should search for them.

Mouse gets up.

                    LUDWIG
          Would they do the same for you?

Mouse considers this, then promptly sits down. He reaches
over to pick up the tome, which has fallen open to a
scene of plague and violence.

Mouse follows the sequence; a great plague afflicting the
village, several adults feeding on a young boy's blood,
and finally, a small girl being placed on an altar.

Mouse mouths the Aramaic passage and his eyes go wide. He
SEES a strange expression on the Old Man's face and
trembles.

INT. CHURCH - NIGHT

Darkness. A gas lamp is lit, revealing Brochauer.
Gottesman fidgets behind him in the entrance.

They gaze in at a scene of demonic proportions; stained
glass windows smashed in, icons with faces burned away
and crosses turned upside down, including a massive
Crucifix behind the altar. Brochauer steps forward in
awe.

                    BROCHAUER
          My God...

Snow drifts through a gaping hole in the ceiling. The
walls are covered in mold and vegetation.

                    GOTTESMAN
               (rocking in place)
          In the fall we grew pumpkin, squash,
          asparagus--

                    BROCHAUER
          It's all right, Gottesman. Don't be
          afraid.

Brochauer heads down the aisle, towards a small door to
the steeple. Gottesman hurries after.

EXT. VILLAGE WALLS - CONTINUOUS

Moonlight falls across Juergen's face, eyes open. He
breath is shallow, blood bubbling from the corner of his
mouth.

Pulling back, we see Uta and Bruno, still feeding at his
torso.

A strange INHUMAN GROAN from above makes the dogs back
off with a WHIMPER, revealing Juergen's intestines.

Juergen's eyes bulge, but he is unable to move.

                    JUERGEN
          No... No... please...!

There is a peculiar SCURRYING from above as something
comes down through the branches at INHUMAN SPEED, rushing
toward Juergen's SCREAMING face.

INT. BELL TOWER - SAME TIME

Brochauer climbs up a tightly winding staircase to a
small door. A few tries and he forces it open.

EXT. LANDING - CONTINUOUS

A single great bell hangs from the tower, nearly rusted
in place by years of disuse. Beside it is a vacant spot
which once held a second one. Brochauer touches the bell
as Gottesman stares out at the full moon.

                    BROCHAUER
          This is the same bell as the one in town.

                    GOTTESMAN
          Bells were introduced to Eastern Europe
          in the 9th century. Bells were often
          baptized before being hung to ward off
          evil spirits, and the sound was thought
          to drive demons away.

Brochauer looks beneath the bell.

                    BROCHAUER
          The ringer's been removed. Who would do
          such a thing? Who would desecrate a
          church like this?

He hears JUERGEN'S DISTANT, ECHOING SCREAMS. His blood
races and he tears back down the tower, Gottesman lagging
behind, SNICKERING.

EXT. VILLAGE SQUARE - MOMENTS LATER

Mouse runs to meet Brochauer and Gottesman at the bell.

                    MOUSE
          Juergen and Dietrich left to find the
          dogs about an hour ago. Since then, I've
          heard screaming from the woods.

                    BROCHAUER
          So did I. We must organize a search--

He starts forward, but Mouse stops him, tome in hand.

                    MOUSE
          There's something you must know first!

Mouse opens the tome and shows it to him.

                    MOUSE (CONT'D)
          There was a plague. See this? It's a
          number written in Aramaic - 1534. The
          year the village was afflicted.

                    BROCHAUER
              (to himself)
          The year on the tombstones.

                    MOUSE
          What tombstones?

                    BROCHAUER
          We found an ancient cemetery. 1534 was
          the latest date.

Mouse flips the page, showing him the adults feeding on
children, then the little girl on the altar.

                    MOUSE
          It started with a child. She spread it to
          the rest of the village. They killed the
          children. All of them.

                    BROCHAUER
          My God.

                    MOUSE
          With my limited knowledge of Aramaic,
          Roma, Albanian... I believe this was not
          only a plague... but a cult!

                    BROCHAUER
          So what does all this mean?

                    MOUSE
          No fresh graves, no farms, no animals,
          ...no children! Only the girl... the
          girl!

                    BROCHAUER
          What are you saying, Mouse? The plague
          was over four centuries ago.

                    MOUSE
          Why do you think she was in the woods
          when we found her? What was she doing?

                    GOTTESMAN
          She was running away from the village.

Brochauer and Mouse look up in surprise, almost
forgetting Gottesman was even there. He smiles shyly.

Brochauer looks towards the cottage in fear.

                    BROCHAUER
          They are still feeding on the flesh of
          their own children!

                    MOUSE
          This book is not only a history. It *is*
          their Bible, a parable of their rise
          after the plague, of how they have
          survived in isolation all these years!
                    (beat)
          The only thing I don't understand is how
          they decide which children shall live and
          which shall die, and why there are almost
          no children now--

A SCREAM interrupts his thought.

                    BROCHAUER
          You must fix that radio!

                    MOUSE
          But the villagers--

                    BROCHAUER
          Arm yourself and protect the girl. It's
          imperative you fix the radio and call for
          help before the storm traps us here. Take
          Gottesman with you and stick together!

                    MOUSE
          And you?

                    BROCHAUER
          I will go to the woods myself.

Mouse takes Gottesman and hurries off.

EXT. VILLAGE WALLS - LATER

Brochauer creeps through the moonlit woods. He HEARS a
STRANGE HOWL nearby.

SQUISH! Brochauer steps in something wet, not snow. He
SNIFFS, something fowl.

He lights a flare and looks down, reeling back in horror
as he sees--

--DIETRICH'S ENTRAILS in the blanched snow, his head the
only recognizable part of him remaining, eyes wide open.

Brochauer drops the flare, its light subdued in the
slush. He lurches forward and VOMITS, then runs back to
the village through the thicket.

EXT. OLD MAN'S COTTAGE - SAME TIME

Mouse and Gottesman arrive at the door. Mouse hands
Gottesman the tome, unslings his rifle and hesitates
before going in.

Gottesman stays outside, handling the tome in wonderment,
BABBLING at the various symbols and pictures.

He hears a HALTED WHISPER from somewhere. GIGGLING, he
follows it to the back of the cottage.

INT. OLD MAN'S COTTAGE - CONTINUOUS

Mouse goes toward the radio, carefully watching the Old
Man, who sits calmly. The Girl is still fevered. Mouse
leans his rifle against the wall and opens up the radio
expertly. He retrieves something from his pocket--

ANGLE ON A CIRCUIT.

                    MOUSE
          Well, here goes my chance to stay out of
          the war altogether...

He puts it in place inside the radio. It immediately
CLICKS ON. He smiles, pressing down a receiver.

                    MOUSE (CONT'D)
          Mayday! Mayday! This is Alpha Bravo
          Romeo! Do you read?

He lifts up on the receiver. A DISTANT SCRATCHING NOISE.

                    MOUSE (CONT'D)
          Mayday! Mayday! This is Alpha Bravo
          Romeo, do you read?

                    BASE STATION (O.S.)
          Alpha Bravo Romeo, this is Army Command
          East. We read you. What are your
          coordinates?

                    MOUSE
          Latitude 41 minutes 25 seconds, longitude
          20 minutes, 25 seconds.

                    BASE STATION
          Copy that... what is your status?

                    MOUSE
          We're caught in enemy territory inside a
          village. We may have had two casualties
          already. We have no supplies, few
          weapons. Over.

                    BASE STATION
          You are in a remote area, Alpha Bravo. We
          can send Mountaineers to you, but it will
          take at least one day. Can you hold out?
          Over.

                    MOUSE
          We have no choice. We'll be waiting.
          Over.

                    BASE STATION
          God be with you. Over and out.

Mouse turns to Ludwig's empty chair.

                    MOUSE
          Ludwig? You sleeping?

He looks at the bedroom doorway. A SHADOW crosses his
face and he starts to turn in relief.

                         MOUSE (CONT'D)
                I knew you were too lazy to go very far--

His expression turns to HORROR as the shadow overcomes
him.

EXT. OLD MAN'S COTTAGE - CONTINUOUS

Behind the cottage, Gottesman stands frozen. Hanging
upside down from a tree before him is Ludwig. His throat
has been cut, blood draining into a large wooden trough.
He TRIES TO SPEAK but all that comes out is a CHOKING
GASP.

Gottesman backs away, clutching the tome to his chest.

                         GOTTESMAN
                Thirteen. The number of participants in
                the last supper. The number of dimensions
                in the Theory of Relativity. The number
                of full moons in a year. According to the
                Torah, God has Thirteen attributes of
                mercy...

GUNSHOTS from the cottage. Gottesman turns and runs.

EXT. VILLAGE ENTRANCE - CONTINUOUS

Brochauer hears the GUNSHOTS and runs into the village.
Hidden in the shadows, Gottesman watches him.

He starts to call out to Brochauer but stops when he sees
several of the Villagers come out of their homes.

Gottesman slips out of the village and into the woods.

EXT. OLD MAN'S COTTAGE - CONTINUOUS

Brochauer carefully approaches the side of the cottage.
He looks into the window and SEES--

Mouse is being drained of blood by --

-- the Girl!

She leans over Mouse, biting into his neck as the Old
Man, and a MALE and FEMALE VILLAGER (30s), hold him down
for her.

The Old Man smiles, revealing ELONGATED CANINES.
VAMPIRES!

                         BROCHAUER
              NO!!!

Brochauer SLAMS his palm on the window pane, CRACKING it.

The Vampires look up at Brochauer and HISS. He turns his
rifle on them, SHATTERING the glass with GUNFIRE. To his
horror, they seem impervious to it, bleeding but
unharmed.

Mouse sees Brochauer and manages to call out.

                         MOUSE
              It's the girl! She's the plague! They
              were only waiting for us to call in more
              troops... for more food!

Brochauer watches in horror as they sink their teeth back
into Mouse. He turns to see several Villagers close the
gates to the village.

                         MOUSE (CONT'D)
              The bell, the tome says they fear the
              bell! Hurry! It's your only hope!!

As Mouse's CRIES are drowned out by their feeding,
Brochauer FIRES uselessly at them.

Realizing he can do nothing more, Brochauer takes aim,
pain in his eyes, and SHOOTS Mouse dead.

The Vampires turn toward Brochauer angrily, their feeding
interrupted. The Girl HISSES.

Brochauer turns to see others coming toward him from
their cottages. He bolts toward the Bell Tower.

EXT. VILLAGE SQUARE - CONTINUOUS

As Brochauer crosses the square the Vampires close in at
inhuman speeds. Desperately, he FIRES his pistol at the
broken bell.

CLANG! The Vampires halt and back away from the noise,
covering their ears as Brochauer runs into the forest.

EXT. CHURCH GRAVEYARD - CONTINUOUS

Brochauer races toward the church. Some of the vampires have torches as they chase him, animalistic in their ability to crawl over every tomb and through the trees.

INT. CHURCH - CONTINUOUS

Brochauer bursts in. The Vampires follow, crawling up the walls and across the ceiling. Brochauer makes an athletic dash for the tower stairwell, barely making it past his pursuers as they hurl themselves toward him.

INT. BELL TOWER - CONTINUOUS

Hordes of demons nip at Brochauer's heels as he climbs to the top and smashes through the door.

INT. LANDING - CONTINUOUS

Brochauer is within inches of death, vampires leaping toward him and crawling up the sides of the steeple, fanged mouths gaping horrifically. He RINGS THE BELL with the butt of his rifle--

CLANG!! The vampires are forced back down the stairwell, SCREECHING, as if struck by a physical blow.

Brochauer SLAMS the door shut and locks it. A moment. Then a mighty PUSH on the door, CRACKING its surface.

Brochauer RINGS THE BELL with the butt of his rifle.

INT. CHURCH - CONTINUOUS

Vampires retreat like insects at the sound of the bell, then slowly creep forward again.

Brochauer keeps RINGING THE BELL. Each time, the Vampires reel in pain, clenching their teeth and covering their ears, but again return for the feeding.

EXT. THE WOODS - DAWN

Gottesman runs towards a small city in the distance. He throws off his army uniform, keeping only the boots, long johns and coat, and continues onward, clutching the tome close.

EXT. LANDING - CONTINUOUS

Brochauer lays on his back, spent and weak, pistol in one
hand, rifle in the other, occasionally RINGING THE BELL.
The Vampires wait for him to tire, their claws
occasionally visible through the cracks in the door.

> BROCHAUER (V.O.)
> How could I blame them? They were only
> surviving like we all were. And like us
> they were members of an unforgivable
> breed, caught in a war they were meant to
> lose. The illusion of immortality is a
> nightmare, yes... perhaps even a plague,
> luring us into a prison of our own
> making. It's only right that I'm here
> with my punishment... a decision to
> either toll the bell until I tire and
> they overcome me, or to turn the gun on
> myself now. But I ring the bell. I'm no
> longer the monster, but the victim. I am
> the Jew, the Gypsy, the Other, caught,
> for now, in the dream of escape, of the
> desperate hope that deep in the core of
> every monster beats a human heart...